Dot.™
UNPLUGGED

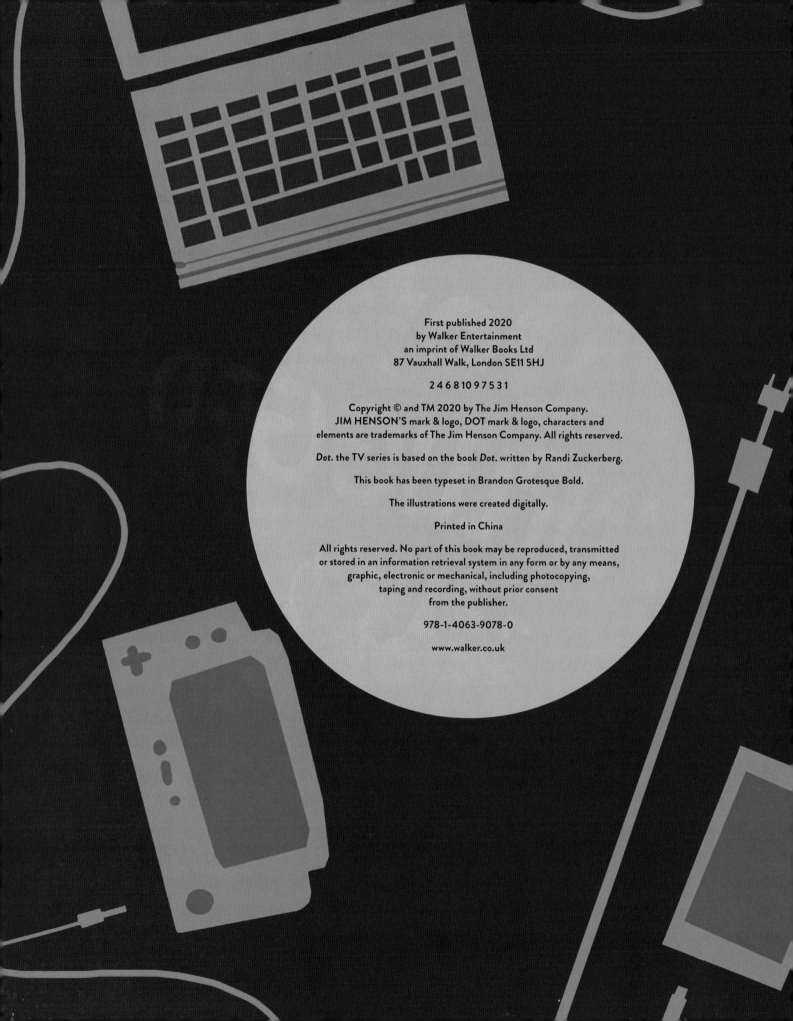

First published 2020
by Walker Entertainment
an imprint of Walker Books Ltd
87 Vauxhall Walk, London SE11 5HJ

2 4 6 8 10 9 7 5 3 1

Dot. the TV series is based on the book *Dot.* written by Randi Zuckerberg.

This book has been typeset in Brandon Grotesque Bold.

The illustrations were created digitally.

Printed in China

978-1-4063-9078-0

www.walker.co.uk

Dot.™

UNPLUGGED

WALKER
ENTERTAINMENT

THE JIM HENSON COMPANY

It was raining. Scratch had his fire engine squeak toy, but he didn't have anyone to play with.

In the living room, Dot and Hal were playing a video game.

Scratch barked.

"Hi, Scratch. Can't play with you right now," said Dot.

"The fate of the universe is at stake!" said Hal.

Scratch ran off.

Scratch found Dad in the kitchen, typing on his computer.

Scratch barked.

"Hey, Scratch," said Dad. "I'm pretty busy right now.
Go find Dot – I think she's in the living room."

Scratch sighed and ran off.

At her worktable, Mum was busy, too.

"Sorry, Scratch, but I have to finish this circuit board."

Scratch whined and plopped down on the floor.

Just then, everything went dark.
The power was out!

"That reminds me! It's National Unplugging Day," said Mum.

"Maybe we should take this as a sign that we should unplug!" said Dad.

Mum told everyone that unplugging meant no electronics – no phones, no computers. "Nothing that runs on anything but our good old imaginations," she said. "What do you say? Should we all unplug until dinner time?"

"I'll set a timer," said Dad.

"Sounds like fun!" said Dot. "What do you think, Hal?"

Hal removed his robot hat. He stepped out of his robot suit.

"I agree to unplug," he said.

"Great!" said Dot. "We can find plenty of things to do inside."

They tried to think of
something to play with.

Drone?

No.

Video games?

Nope.

Keyboard?

It's electric.

Tablet?

Same same.

"Unplugging is harder than I thought," said Dot, "especially when you can't go outside."

Mum was heading to the basement to put the lights back on.
Dad, Dot and Hal tagged along, determined to stay unplugged.

"Boy, there's a lot of stuff down here," said Hal.

They found old clothes, an easel, paints, Dot's craft box, clay and pipe cleaners – even tap shoes!

Then Scratch pulled something out of an old, dusty box.

"The spinner game!" said Dot.

"How do you play?" asked Hal.

"You spin, and then you have to do the task that you land on," Dot said. "Let's play!"

Hal went first. The pointer landed on the bird.

"You have to sing a song," said Dot, "in a bird's voice."

Hal chirped a song.

"'The Itsy-Bitsy Spider'?" asked Dad.

Everyone laughed. Hal wouldn't sing a spider song.
He hated spiders.

"'The Farmer in the Dell'!" said Mum. That was it!

Mum went next. She had to make something.
She crafted a calculator out of clay and buttons.

Dad had to play charades. He pretended to surf.
Then he pretended to be a spider. No one got it.

"Surfing the web!" he said.

Dot took her turn. She had to search for something – something with an engine.

She looked around.

Squeak!

Aha! Scratch had just the thing. The fire engine toy. Good dog, Scratch!

They played all
afternoon.

Until...

DING!

The timer rang.

"Let's keep playing!"
said Dot. "Unplugging
is fun!"

Get the Unplugged Bug!

Whether you decide to unplug once a week, once a month,
or once a year, here are fifty ideas to disconnect
from your devices and reconnect with yourself,
your family and your friends.

PUT PENCIL TO PAPER

- Write your own secret code
- Write a knock-knock joke
- Write a silly story
- Write a newspaper article
- Write a comic strip
- Write a poem
- Write a song
- Write a play based on your favourite book

FUN AND GAMES

- Play charades
- Play a board game
- Play cards
- Play a memory game
- Play "I Spy"

BE AN ARTIST AND MAKE STUFF

- Make jewellery from recyclables
- Draw or paint a portrait of your pet
- Make a bird feeder
- Make a postcard and send it
- Make a sculpture from found objects
- Make your own playing cards
- Draw a picture outside with chalk
- Make a musical instrument
- Make a paper aeroplane
- Draw or paint a self-portrait
- Create an art project from things found in nature
- Make your own play dough
- Make a puppet
- Make an ice or snow art project

EXPLORE

- Go on a scavenger hunt
- Identify a bird
- Find a constellation in the night sky
- List 5 animals you've seen near your house
- Interview a parent or grandparent about your family history
- Draw a treasure map

QUIET TIME

- Read a book!
- Meditate
- Do yoga
- Find out about volunteer opportunities in your community

LEARN SOMETHING NEW

- Learn a card trick
- Learn pig Latin
- Learn to knit
- Learn 10 words in a new language

MORE UNPLUGGED THINGS TO DO

- Make a time capsule
- Make a word search puzzle
- Plan and cook a meal for your family
- Plant an indoor garden
- Plant an outdoor garden
- Have a picnic
- Hold a silly face contest
- Build an indoor den
- Build an outdoor den